Margriet Ruurs

COME, READ WITH ME

illustrated by Christine Wei

ORCA BOOK PUBLISHERS

Come, let's read.

Cuddle closer, open your eyes.
Let's look at the pictures and fly through the skies.

The adventures on these pages are as old as the ages,
so let's read...
Let's read big books and small, new books and old.
I promise the best tales you've ever been told.

Together we'll travel to faraway lands

where spiders weave words and animals talk.

All we need is this book that we hold in our hands.

We'll meet fairies and gnomes and magical things,
soar high in the air on dragon wings.

Now turn the page and look at each word...

The best spells that you've ever heard!

These stories sound like wind in the willows.
Just follow my voice and fluff up your pillows.

Hold-on tight to my hand
as we sail away to Neverland.

I spot pirates and treasure on a faraway shore
of an island dotted with coconut trees,
parrots who screech as monkeys swing
in the breeze.

Read on, there is so much more
to explore!

Oh, look! Look at that fluke—it's the tale of a whale!

And a jungle of wild things who march to their very own beat.

Oh, the places we'll go, the things you will meet.

Waves of words take us back to the shore.

Quick, turn that page—let's read on some more.

All these squiggly lines are just made of ink,
but they make us imagine and make us think.

What if you were a king and I were a queen?
We'd live in the biggest castle you've ever seen!

There's a yellow brick road that leads out of town.
Put on your glass slippers and straighten your crown.
Let's follow these breadcrumbs into the wood.
We'll go visit our friend in a red riding hood.

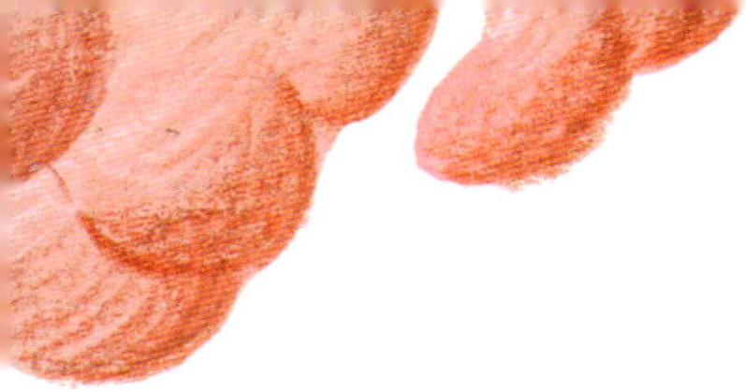

But wait! A house made of candy?
Let's take a nibble while we watch
wicked stepsisters quibble.

(Who *is* going to the ball?)

And there is an egg perched on a wall,
sitting next to a princess who is yawning with grace
and watching a hare and a turtle who race.

And you, stay awake, though I know that it's late
and it's hard to keep all these characters straight—
but do you hear that? Do you hear that sound?
Let's keep on going to see what we've found.

It's a pied piper and his haunting tune.
By the light of the stars and the magical moon,
we'll march with a puss in boots and a cat in a hat
behind a proud lion and a grumpy rat.

A girl who has pigtails walks with a horse.
There are plenty of princes and a peacock, of course.
Make way for a duckling and a big furry dog,
and wish for a good knight while kissing a frog.

And when we get tired, you'll sit and drink tea
with a friend, her white rabbit and, of course, me!

The wolf comes along to steal a bite from our table.
Let's be kind and invite him to hear this fine fable.

These books hold a promise as old as the ages.
Our happily ever after will be found in these pages.

Come, cuddle closer...now close your eyes.
The story is finished, and the moon's on the rise.

Goodnight, little readers. *Sleep tight.*

In memory of Dashdondog and for Basarat,
who knows the power of stories.
—M.R.

To my beloved parents and sister, who never to my knowledge attempted to trade me for a less crazy child, and encouraged my dream with patience and love.
—C.W.

Published in Canada and the United States in 2021 by Orca Book Publishers.
orcabook.com

Library and Archives Canada Cataloguing in Publication
Title: Come, read with me / Margriet Ruurs; illustrated by Christine Wei.
Names: Ruurs, Margriet, author. | Wei, Christine, illustrator.
Identifiers: Canadiana (print) 20200331566 | Canadiana (ebook) 20200331574 | ISBN 9781459817876 (hardcover) | ISBN 9781459817883 (PDF) | ISBN 9781459817890 (EPUB)
Classification: LCC PS8585.U97 C66 2021 | DDC jC813/.54—dc23

Library of Congress Control Number: 2020944969

Summary: In this picture book about stories and reading, contemporary children are whisked through an imaginary world while interacting with characters from classic fairy tales.

Orca Book Publishers is committed to reducing the consumption of nonrenewable resources in the making of our books. We make every effort to use materials that support a sustainable future.

Orca Book Publishers gratefully acknowledges the support for its publishing programs provided by the following agencies: the Government of Canada, the Canada Council for the Arts and the Province of British Columbia through the BC Arts Council and the Book Publishing Tax Credit.

Cover and interior artwork created with mixed media on printmaking paper, such as watercolor, gouache, pastel, charcoal, collage and finalized with some digital enhancements.

Cover and interior artwork by Christine Wei
Edited by Liz Kemp
Design by Rachel Page

Printed and bound in China.

24 23 22 21 • 1 2 3 4

Margriet Ruurs is the author of forty books for children, many of which are award-winning titles, including *Stepping Stones: A Refugee Family's Journey*, which won the Bolen Books Children's Book Prize and has been translated into eight languages. Margriet's love of reading and writing children's books was nurtured from an early age through fairy tales and poetry. She works with teachers, parents and children in schools around the world, conducting writing workshops and author presentations. Margriet lives on Salt Spring Island, British Columbia.

Born in Taiwan and currently based in Vancouver, *Christine Wei* has a bachelor of fine arts with a major in illustration from the Emily Carr University of Art + Design. Christine's works are often inspired by and about the natural, social and cultural landscapes around her, and she incorporates nature-inspired patterns in the landscapes and objects she paints.